Dawn's Cozy Horror Corner

A queer Chinese diaspora horror short stories anthology

Dawn Chen

Published by Dawn Chen

Cover Design by 麻辣月亮

Interior Formatting by @ValleyAndVale

ISBN 978-1-7384917-0-4 (paperback)

ISBN 978-1-7384917-1-1 (ebook)

Content Warnings

Bottle of Shame
Sexual assault (including implied SA of a minor), rape, gore.
The Girl with No Face
Bullying, gore, racism.
My Future Self Once Said
Suicide (attempted), suicide ideation, drug overdose, self-harm.
Judge of the Underworld Household
Mild gore.
Meet Your Demons
Insomnia, demonic possession, depressive and borderline suicidal thoughts.

Bottle of Shame

Wu Yan was seven when she first discovered she had the power to physically pull out other people's bottled-up shame.

Shame took the physical form of green goo and grime. It coursed through one's veins and stuck to one's skin. They became you, and you became them.

The first person from whom Yan pulled shame was her childhood best friend.

Her best friend was like the sun. She wore a white dress dotted with yellow flower petals. Her blonde hair glittered in golden threads. Her hazel eyes sparkled under the sun, distant planets radiating light.

Yan must have been jealous of her; it was hard to remember but not that hard to make sense of. As the child of Chinese immigrant parents, she longed for the confidence of her best friend who seemed so at home. Her friend had all the attention no matter where she went. She was the kind of child who stole everyone's heart with her charms.

The golden girl that was her best friend could have used her loveliness to get anything she wanted. At an age when children were self-centred and moral compasses were still nowhere to be seen, her best friend could have been mean and cruel. Yet, she was sweet as cotton candy and gentle as an ocean breeze. She never joked about the shape of Yan's eyes or her accent.

It was that fairytale girl who went home every day to an uncle who touched her at all the places he shouldn't have.

Yan didn't understand. She couldn't comprehend how this could happen to someone like her best friend, the friend who had never hurt a single fly, who was the epitome of childhood innocence.

Her best friend didn't change profoundly. The bright little girl still shone like the sun. Her kind nature was never eaten away by the growing shadow behind her eyes. The only difference was that she would be less talkative in the classes of their male teachers. She would clutch Yan's elbows like a lifeline whenever it was her uncle's turn to pick her up. Maybe it was because she didn't yet understand what she went through. Maybe she was afraid of her parents getting mad if they knew.

They told each other everything. Yan must have confided in her friend before it all went wrong. They were sitting back to back on a yellow carpet that matched her friend's dress. Hand in hand.

Yan had just shared a secret with her friend, so her friend told her one in return.

The next thing Yan knew, her best friend was puking teal green grime all over the carpet floor.

They were sitting in Yan's room, somewhere private and safe. Maybe that was why her best friend thought she could even be allowed to feel her shame. But it wasn't enough, since the endless green goo pouring out of her best friend was leaking through the floor.

Yan's parents came up to see what was wrong and were horrified by the swamp flood coming out of Yan's best friend's mouth.

At some point, Yan's best friend started crying, and her face turned from green to red like the lights on a Christmas tree. Back then, Yan didn't know that the green liquid was the physical manifestation of shame. All she understood was that she had made her friend very, very upset.

Yan told Mum and Dad what had happened as they called her best friend's parents to pick the girl up. Her parents were horrified by Yan's tale, which included what her best friend had said about her uncle. They spoke in muffled tones in the living room when her friend's parents came to pick her up.

Tears were shed. Words were said. Doors were slammed.

Yan never saw her best friend again. She never got to know if it was her parents who decided it was the end to their friendship, or if it was because the girl's parents didn't want her to play with Yan after that.

Yan only knew that she was cut out of her best friend's life after that fateful day when she discovered her superpower. It was a lot like Spiderman, just harder to clean up.

She wondered if the girl's parents did something about her best friend's uncle. She didn't fully understand what was going on, but it made her best friend who was always laughing so incredibly sad. Then it couldn't be good, right?

The only trace that reminded Yan of her best friend was the dark stain left on the yellow carpet. No matter how hard her parents tried, they couldn't scrub it off.

The second person whom Yan pulled shame out of was her cousin.

It was during the winter holiday when Yan took a plane back home. The cold in Beijing was a knife that pierced into one's skull, unapologetic and determined. Even if one was fully armed with down jackets and sweaters and scarves, one could still lose a finger or an ear to the numbing air.

Filled with ambition and potential, Yan's cousin was a child of Beijing in every sense of that title.In a city that never slept and that prided itself on hard work, her cousin studied hard at night and always won awards. Her future was as cold as the winter, but she was the knife that would cut through the ice even if it killed her.

Almost every parent in their city had a tutor for their children outside of school. It had very little to do with the child's competency and everything to do with giving the child a step up in the merciless competition that was the annual district grade ranking. This was seen not as something voluntary, but mandatory. Almost every single child under the age of eighteen would go to tutoring outside of their Monday to Friday schooling. That was simply the norm.

Yan stepped outside and saw her cousin, the same young girl who was the pride and joy of their family. She stood straight like a tree. Her long branches stretched to embrace Yan, the little bird who had been far away from the nest for too long.

Yan fell into her cousin's arms. It was then that turquoise droplets started to replace the cold sweat on her cousin's forehead.

The happy reunion should have prompted laughter and contentment. But her cousin was frozen. Green grime dripped from her eyes and oozed from her pores. The sour taste of the liquidated shame attracted onlookers' attention. People whispered all around them.

Yan's uncle rushed closer to their withered daughter who kept bleeding emerald goo. Her aunt's eyes darted from left to right, anxiously trying to observe if anyone had discovered the secret behind the shame that was eating up her daughter from the inside out.

Yan's parents turned their faces away. Her mother told Yan that it was her cousin's family business. It was drawing attention, so it was wrong.

The adults appeared so practised in their reactions. That was when Yan realised: they all knew. Her superpower told her the whole story. They all knew what her cousin had been holding inside for so long.

Yan's cousin didn't puke all of her shame out in one go like her best friend. Instead, the green grime replaced the water in her cousin's body. It seeped into the girl's skin like a sponge sucking in water. After every tutoring session, her cousin's blood was replaced a little bit more with that green goo.

Until one day, all her cousin's tears and sweat that came out reeked of the unspeakable shame.

Later, Yan asked her cousin why she didn't tell someone. She asked her cousin why she didn't stop going to the same tutor.

Her cousin answered Yan saying that Goakao was close. Her parents had paid too much money to the tutor in advance for her to stop going. Also, who could she tell?

Yan didn't understand. She couldn't comprehend how this could happen to someone like her cousin, the cousin who appeared strong and unrelenting, who was never supposed to be a victim.

After that, Yan accidentally pulled out green grime more and more frequently. Day in and day out.

She could accidentally bump into a pedestrian. The pedestrian's hair would suddenly be filled with oozing green dots.

She could high-five her teammates after a football match. The teammate would suddenly collapse with their hand going up in green smoke.

She could have her favorite teacher patting her shoulder approvingly. The teacher would stop smiling and run toward the loo.

Yan still didn't understand. There was no logic behind any of it, no way to trace when the shame would explode and who the shame would belong to.

Yan wished someone could tell her when a person walked past who was filled with pain. Yan wanted some indication that could inform her of what to say and what to do. Surely she could do something with this power.

Yan came clean to her mum about her powers. She asked for her mum's help because there was no question that her mother didn't have an answer to.

Her mum sighed. She wrapped her hands around Yan's shoulders. For a second, Yan closed her eyes, imagining that she was finally safe from harm.

When Yan opened her eyes and looked into the face of her mother, her mum was smiling with green grime staining her tongue.

"Yan, there is no way you could help," Yan's mum told her softly.

"It happened to me. It happened to my mum as well. And the mum of your grandma. You're lucky that it never happened to you. All you can do is to stop it from happening to yourself."

Yan stopped making physical contact with people altogether.

Wherever she went from then on, the green grime and goo haunted her like a ghost.

At some point, Yan forgot how it felt to speak her mind in the middle of a crowd. She stopped going with her parents to their Tuesday family dinner. She stopped playing football because of the close contact with others. She stopped hanging out with her friends in shopping centres. She stopped opening her mouth.

Every time Yan was in the middle of a pleasant conversation with someone, the dark stain that was stuck on her carpet floor would emerge and mute out all the laughter in the world.

The people she was in a conversation with were left behind, lost, and dumbfounded. Every time Yan wanted to apologise, all she could see was how the bystanders at the airport turned their heads away as the liquidated shame came out of her cousin's body like a broken water tank.

The second to last person whom Yan pulled shame out of was her roommate.

Somehow despite her avoidance of all human interactions, Yan still made it into university. She thought she forgot how to smile until her roommate taught her how to.

Her roommate was like the autumn leaves gently tumbling to the ground. She never forced Yan to talk when Yan's head was filled with ugly thoughts. Her roommate, who always brought a second box of food home for her. Her roommate, who rubbed Yan's back and whispered in her ears when she was having a panic attack.

Her roommate, who was there when Yan needed a friend. Her roommate, who listened to Yan's tales and believed her every word. Her roommate, who knew all about shame because she had to hide her sexuality from her family for years.

Her roommate had a wonderful relationship with another girl. They made Yan believe in love again. They brought Yan to parties and movies. Yan met her boyfriend through them.

One day, her roommate and Yan went to a party with a bunch of their friends. They all had a lot to drink. Yan had not felt so at home for a long time. She lost her footing once or twice as the world swirled around.

She should have kept an eye out for her roommate. She should have recognized the uncomfortable looks her roommate was giving a boy who was there with them. A boy who didn't back down even after her roommate told him that she was a lesbian.

Yan didn't look out for her roommate because she was blackout drunk. She would regret her decision forever.

The next day, Yan and her roommate took turns puking in the washroom. Amid the yellow and brown bile mixed with the smell of alcohol, greenish taint shimmered like grasses being swept away in an avalanche.

Her roommate's eyes drilled at the loo. As if she stared long enough at the shimmering green, what happened the night before would become just a bad dream.

The boy was in the same course as Yan's roommate. She went to lectures and seminars in the same space as her rapist. It went on like that for another year until her roommate transferred to another university.

Her roommate never reported what happened to the authorities, because years before there was a rape chat scandal at the very same university. The people involved were banned from the university for less than a year; they came back while the girls they threatened were still studying on the same campus.

There it was, the people in the airports who turned away from Yan's cousin's shame. They were there at her university as well.

The last person Yan pulled the shame out of was herself.

On the day of graduation, Yan walked onto the stage to accept her undergraduate degree. She tried her best to hold in all the things that were boiling underneath. She swallowed the puke that was squirming in her throat. Yan did not doubt what colour the sizzling emotions would take.

Yan stood there and looked down. All these young women and men, the future of this country.

How many of them had the green grime running through them at this moment? she thought. How many of them would taste it in the future?

Yan saw a small girl wearing a white dress with yellow flowers. She must have been another graduate's little sister or daughter. Was she safe?

Yan saw her cousin standing next to her parents and smiling at her . She was in a black suit with her hair combed back. Her cousin had become the skilled doctor all those tutoring sessions helped to pave the way to. Was it enough?

Yan saw her roommate holding a bouquet, who had just driven hours here after her own graduation ceremony. Her girlfriend was nowhere to be found. Did that have anything to do with what happened?

All of their faces caught up in Yan's mind, slowly blending into one. One filled with all the shame ever inflicted on every single victim of such pain since the dawn of time. A green dripping silhouette that was filled with regret.

Yan closed her eyes. She held her hand out towards the green silhouette.

In front of all the people in the auditorium. Wu Yan exploded into a million pieces of grime and goo.

The girl who pulled out shame became the girl who was made out of shame. Her blood was teal and her sinew turquoise. Her eyes rolled to the ground like two emerald stones. Her hair turned to strings of grass, and her fingernails burst into small puddles of moss.

People screamed and scattered.

At least they finally couldn't look away from the shame.

The Girl with No Face

Jia Si Ya started with all the facial features a normal human would have. Two ears, one mouth, two eyes, and a nose.

She was a normal sort of girl growing up in China. Quiet, artistic, and most importantly, her grades are always among the top three in her class. She was left alone to her own devices because you simply don't mess with a girl who has good grades in China. The teachers were always on her side. She was not close to most of her classmates; they'd look at her with some jealousy, but that was plenty made up by their reverence for her good grades. She had one or two close friends who knew her like they knew themselves.

Then, one day, her parents set her down and told her they were getting on an airplane. They packed their three-room apartment into ten plastic boxes. They caught a taxi to the airport. That is how Jia Si Ya ended up in a land where night is day and day is night.

Jia Si Ya began to lose parts of her body on the first day of school.

"Everyone, this is a new student, her name is…"

The teacher's face scrunched up into a walnut, filled with lines. She looked like she had eaten something wrong.

"Jia Si Ya," she said sincerely. "It's Jia-Si-Ya."

All her new classmates stayed silent. Some of their faces scrunched up like walnuts too. Suddenly, Jia Si Ya was standing in front of a classroom of walnuts.

"Do you have an English name?" The teacher approached her carefully as if speaking to a sleeping lion rather than a small girl.

"No," Jia Si Ya replied. "I'm not English."

That made the class laugh. Not the sort of laugh Jia Si Ya is used to from her old classmates. It had a strange tone to it, as if there was poison mixed with honey.

The teacher shook her head as if Jia Si Ya just admitted she kicked someone off the cliff. "Well, you'll need one from now on. You'll be Jane. A pretty name."

Jia Si Ya didn't reply. She wanted to ask the teacher who she was to give her a name when she already had one. The teacher had simply thrown a name at her, as if she were a stray kitten the teacher just picked up from the streets.

Jia Si Ya lost an ear that day because she didn't want to hear the name that she did not claim. Everyone called her that one-syllable word from then on. Jia Si Ya always walked away without answering their words as they screamed at her from down the hall.

Her classmates slowly realised that Jia Si Ya was purposefully ignoring them. They took personal offence with that, as children always do. They thought that Jia Si Ya was the newcomer, the outsider, the one who didn't look like anyone else.

"Why is that girl not talking to us?" they asked their parents.

"She probably just doesn't know how to speak English," their parents answered patiently.

The next day when the classmates came back to school, they repeated the exact words their parents told them to Jia Si Ya.

"You cannot speak English, can you?" They said, "That is why you don't answer us."

"What?" Jia Si Ya sputtered in indignation. "No, I learned English when I was a child. I just don't like to talk much. I like books."

The classmates laughed with delight. "She couldn't speak English."

"I am literally speaking English with you right now."

"*I am literally speaking English with you right now!*" The children chanted, with a twisty and shrill voice as if they were singing in the opera.

Jia Si Ya lost another ear that day. She would not listen to any more of this nonsense; she would not give them any ammunition. So she shed her ears as if they were some bad skin. From then on she had to hear no more.

When Jia Si Ya could no longer hear, she spent her days in the library reading books. Books about love and death. Books about friendship and happiness. Books about magic. Jia Si Ya thought she must have a certain kind of magic, too. She had never seen anyone else who could shed parts of themselves without pain or anyone noticing.

The only person who noticed she had no ears was the librarian, a kind older woman with dreadlocks. She never tried to speak to Jia Si Ya because she noticed Jia Si Ya had no ears, so instead the librarian communicated with her in writing.

The old librarian had the most beautiful handwriting. Her words looked like butterflies that could open their wings and fly away. Jia Si Ya tried to imitate the old librarian's handwriting at home, but the scribbles that came out from her childish hands were just ugly turtles.

The librarian gave books to Jia Si Ya with different kinds of people in them. Some had the librarian's skin colour, and some spoke Jia Si Ya's language. Some whose brain functioned differently and some who lost body parts like Jia Si Ya. Some with girls kissing girls and boys kissing boys. Some with protagonists who don't like kissing at all.

"It's important," the librarian wrote to Jia Si Ya. "Stories are a reflection of the world. Only when our stories rightfully reflect all kinds of people in the world, then stories can become real."

Jia Si Ya thought of that often. She thought that her classmates and her teacher possibly had magic, too, since they saw a different world than the reality the librarian and Jia Si Ya lived in. Her classmates and her teachers only see the world of their own, where every single person is like themselves.

One day, the principal came and told the librarian to go home. The librarian had been trying to fill the library with books that reflect the real world. The principal said the parents didn't like that. He said the parents thought the librarian was trying to cause a fracture in their beautiful, imaginary world.

The librarian was gone the next morning. She left behind a note on Jia Si Ya's locker. "Never forget to keep reading," it said.

Jia Si Ya nodded and kept the note inside her pencil case. Her mouth peeled off like a worn sticker. It was useless, anyway. There was no use for a mouth when no one wanted to hear what you had to say.

A birthday party for one of the most popular girls of their year was swiftly approaching. She came up to a mouthless and earless Jia Si Ya one day, handing her an invitation to the party. Jia Si Ya stood there, not understanding at first. Since she had no ears or a mouth, she couldn't understand what they were saying to her, nor could she give a reply.

However, at the end of the day, Jia Si Ya went home and read the letter. She wanted to scream in joy at seeing the words on the invitation. This was the first time she was welcomed to a party. She wanted to be fully prepared.

She even asked her mother how to do eye makeup. Her mother, who was a model when they were back in China, happily obliged. Her mother was always busy keeping the family afloat in this foreign country, as the dream they were promised was not nearly as good as reality. She noticed her daughter gradually losing facial features, but the mom just assumed her daughter had misplaced them.

"They'll come back," the mother told herself. "Once Si Ya is a little older, they'll grow back."

Jia Si Ya went to the party, with a heart filled with hope. She couldn't hear the music blasting, but she could smell the stench of alcohol. It made her throat perk up, unlike the cool kids in school. She had never tried alcohol.

The birthday girl led Jia Si Ya into a different room away from everyone. She whispered something to Jia Si Ya that she didn't understand. But Jia Si Ya wasn't stupid, and from the body language of the girl, Jia Si Ya understood that she wanted Jia Si Ya to stay in this room because there was a surprise for her.

Jia Si Ya was thinking how kind this all was. It was the girl's birthday, but she was making a surprise for Jia Si Ya? That was so thoughtful and sweet.

She waited. The girl came back and led Jia Si Ya back into the room where everyone was.

Jia Si Ya blinked. All the students that were there had their eyes taped into a line. She could see veins popping up from where the tape stretched skin into the corner. You could barely see their eyeballs; all one could see was a thin line of red tissue.

Jia Si Ya didn't say a thing as the entire room of students stared her down as if they were expecting her to laugh.

Her eyes peeled away from her face. The second eye to drop to the ground still had a single tear on its surface before it evaporated.

All Jia Si Ya had left was her nose.

Her nose was great. Despite not having any other facial features anymore, Jia Si Ya cherished her nose as if it were a piece of treasure. She loved all the smells of the world. The grass after a rainy day. An old book with pages turning yellow. Pu'er tea that was her mom's favourite.

Most importantly, the lunch was filled with Jing Cai (cuisine of Beijing) her parents always packed for her. Eggplant sauce noodles, Beijing barbeque, beef dipped in a special sauce for days on end just for that particular flavour. One time after her parents had a gathering dinner with all their Chinese friends, her mom even took some leftover Beijing roast duck with her to school.

That was the day her classmate took her lunch box. They had always been holding their fingers on their nose whenever Jia Si Ya opened her lunch box or made sputtering sounds. But that day, they went a little bit further.

They snatched the lunch box from Jia Si Ya's grip. Because she had no eyes or ears, Jia Si Ya didn't see or hear them coming. Because she had no mouth, Jia Si Ya couldn't scream or tell them to stop.

The only sensation left was a tingling sense in her nostril. As the rich smell of the roast duck ready for consumption mixed up with the odour of old trash. The rotten banana skin, the scrunched-up tissue papers filled with someone's coughed-up saliva, the stench of chewed-up gum. All of that turned into a gigantic monster and swallowed up the delicious roasted duck.

Jia Si Ya's nose slipped away like the last feather of a bird. It dropped to the ground, leaving raw pink skin and a flat surface behind.

Her classmates stopped laughing. They only now noticed that Jia Si Ya has no features left on her face.

The screams filled the school. No one came out of there when school ended that day. Not the next day or the day after.

Rumor has it, even now when you step onto the haunted grounds of that school, you can still possibly encounter a girl with no face.

If you ever do see her, you better hope that you are not the kind of person who took away other people's faces, or she will take yours because you made her insecure about hers.

My Future Self Once Said

"You'll never know unless you try."

She tried to convince herself as she stared into the pills in the container. All of them reflected ghastly white light in the washroom.

Her legs felt numb as she tangled them together to fit into the small space next to the shower. She didn't want to stand up and look into the mirror and see her face.

The motions wouldn't be that hard. All she needed to do was to crack open the lid and swallow those little white tablets, like how she swallowed the brown marbles in a bubble tea. Except for the difference of being chewy and sweet, the pills would taste bitter and solid.

They might all stick in the middle of her throat, forming a conglomerate of white goo that is solid in the middle and choke her while screaming the accusation:

"Why did you choose to kill yourself? How dare you? Why? Why? Why?"

She wrestled away the urge to answer that question. All the

ones she used to give never came to fruition: parents are cruel or absent, her peers' bullying, her teachers ignoring her, racial slurs, her mental illness, her therapist not working, this medication not working. Nothing worked.

All those answers used to seem so big as they crushed onto her head one by one, but now they barely seemed heavier than a droplet of rain. The only thing that was left was that black hole inside that pumped out despair.

That hole ate away at everything she was — and nothing satisfied its hunger. In the beginning, it only made prey out of the good things she had in life. Like friends, or her enjoyment of reading a book, or drawing, or imagining a fantasy world inside her head. Sooner than later, the scale tipped until all the happiness was digested by the black hole's stomach.

Then, every single thing in life turned sour. Being rejected from her dream university, fighting with the only friend she left back home in a foreign land, her visa running out as she reached adulthood. Nowhere on the map provided an answer on where to go next.

With all that in mind, the black hole took over. It ate away the pain and anxiety and only left one possibility. She was destined to be eaten by the hole, too. Because nothing else was left of her, so at least she needed a way to find peace.

"You'll never know unless you try," she repeated to herself as she tried to stop her trembling lips. Her hand holding the bottle got closer and closer to her mouth. It might not hurt. It might just be like falling asleep. It might finally be the solution to all of her problems.

"Yes, but have you tried?"

That voice startled her enough that she let out a little yelp. She cracked open the lid and one or two tablets fell through the cracks and hit the floor with little bouncy noises, like the chuckles of a child.

"What the fuck?" The last shambles of her that weren't gobbled down by the black hole exclaimed in shock.

Who could be here at this time? She made sure the timing was correct so that no one would be at home except for herself. Plus, the washroom lock was locked for a reason. She didn't even hear the turning of a door handle.

"Oh, sorry." The intruder who was now taking up half of the limited space of the washroom apologised quickly. The intruder was a short woman with hair just long enough to be tied into a ponytail, black as the night and soft as silk. She wore a white blouse and a brown long skirt, coupled with a long beige jacket.

"Didn't mean to scare you. Was just nervous. Thought I was a few seconds too late and broke the time loop. And, you know, erase my existence because you really went through with it."

A fashionable burglar — that was the first impression her boggled mind had come up with. Until the intruder tilted her head and looked at her straight in the eyes.

The intruder had the same face as her, only fewer scratches and chapped lips left behind by habits she developed as anxiety grew in her like a paradisical flower.

She'd yell, *"Who the fuck are you?"* but even that required energy. Left with none, she only stared and blinked at the individual who claimed her face.

"Who ... what are you?"

§The intruder's face glowed under the pale light that was supposed to witness her doom. The shape of her face was devoid of the last of baby fat and the bags that grew under her eyes. It was her, but a decade older. How was this possible?

"Ah," herself from the future blinked and said. *"This is awkward, but judging by the expression on our face, you're already realising who I am."*

"My face," she replied instinctually.

"Fair enough," the woman said with a wave of her hand. *"It is*

yours for now. It was mine in the past. One day, you'll have my face too. If you live to see it."

She was still startled, but this situation was bizarre enough that even the black hole had stopped its gluttonous consumption and settled down to listen.

A million questions flew through her mind, but only one tumbled out of her mouth audibly.

"Why do you talk like a mad philosophy professor?"

"Wow, rude," the woman, her future self, whatever she was, exclaimed in indignation.

"Was I such an asshole at this age?" The woman stared at her up and down like a paleontologist inspecting a dinosaur specimen. *"I mean, I remember by the end I felt like I won't last much longer, so I might as well push everyone in my life away so it hurt less when the suicide plan sails through ... That would explain this."*

Despite everything, she still felt offended by this clear display of judgement.

"What do you mean by *this*?" She gestured at herself, up and down. Wrinkled clothes, unbrushed hair, tear-stained sleeves. Okay, she might have been a big sad sack of potatoes that was ready to die, but who the heck did this woman think she was to stand there and judge her? "I can hear you."

"Sorry." The woman bowed with no ounce of regret in her voice. *"I forgot that at your age I was sensitive and was still in a mental health shithole. It's funny how our memories select which part of our lives to remember, isn't it? This part was sad, so I just kind of forgot about what you were like."*

"Erh, I'm literally standing right here listening to you insult me," she said in a monotone as the black hole ate away the colourful notes of her voice, too. "Apologies not accepted. Also, are you supposed to be like ... the future me?"

The woman finally looked up at her as if seeing a person instead of an interesting scientific discovery. *"Oh no, I'm just one of the infinite amount of future us. Uses, or is it Us'ses? Fuck, the grammar is weird when it comes to different timelines and pluralizing yourself, especially because I study Horology. English is just wrong as a language, I think that's the only thing you and I might agree on. That part hasn't changed. This language is wack when it comes to grammar."*

"Horology?" She thought she probably had just lost her mind.

"Yeah," the woman finally seemed to register her slowly crumbling distraught. Her future self's features softened. *"Sorry, I forgot. You are in pain, aren't you? I remember us trying to end our life, but I don't remember how the pain actually felt. A bitter dosage of Chinese medicine grandma used to boil in the pot? Or a crushing mountain of weight that buries you under?"*

No one has ever asked her that. Not her parents, not her friends, not even the overpriced therapist she saw once a week.

"A black hole," she murmured the answer in a quiet voice. "A black hole that eats everything away."

"Yes," the woman's face contorted as if someone was stirring the peaceful surface of a lake and trying to reach a fallen coin underneath. *"A black hole. That's right."*

"So you remember?" she asked with a dulled surprise. Ever since the black hole came by, the whole world swam instead of focusing on solid ground. "Then how come you're still here?"

Did she not go through with it? Did this mean she never had the resolve even as she knew this was the only way out? Did this mean she survived somehow, found by one of her family members who pretended to care and panicked? Did this mean awkward hospital visits and questions about why she did it? Did this mean even as she finally, *finally* dared to hop out of this life where she screwed up everything, there was still no end to the black hole inside her?

"No, no, no." Her future self's voice dragged her back out. *"No to all those questions that are overwhelming your little brain, past-me. You would have gone through with it, believe me. And you'd die as you wish. The*

only reason you didn't is because I interfered by creating a time paradox where I show you there is a reason to live on."

"That makes about zero sense," she replied. "No offence, but seeing you as my future is not really convincing enough for me to change my mind."

"Oof, offence taken." Her future self shook her head in disbelief. *"How about you hear me out, kid? I'm not the only possible future self of yours. There are a trillion different timelines that will diverge from here on out. We are all versions of you extending beyond this point of time. I'm just the one from the timeline where you chose to apprentice with a time-travelling wizard and the one who stopped you from killing us all."*

"Why?" she asked, confused. "Also, *time-travelling wizard?*"

"Yeah, I'm the coolest version of your future timelines." She could not believe the woman just *winked* at her. *"But that's beside the point. You won't kill yourself, because that means you'll technically be killing me. And I know part of this whole downward spiral suicidal thought business of ours thought that it's the best way out without hurting anyone. It makes zero sense. Back then, though, it seemed to be the only way."*

"I would ... kill you?" She pointed her finger at the woman, a version of herself that looked polished as if created by the Goddess of Beauty, Venus herself. "If I kill myself?"

"Yes." The woman nodded seriously.

She couldn't help but believe her.

"All of us. The one where you went back home to Beijing and bought a two-bedroom apartment with your girlfriend. The one where you got to do a creative writing degree and eventually publish your book. The one that you got possessed by a supernatural being and now consults ghosts for a living. Me, the one who learned the magic of time travel so that your story doesn't just end here and instead moves on to become something more."

"I can't," she said as the black hole flared up every time. It did so each time her future self spoke of a different future—after all, she was not supposed to have a future. "This pain is too much. There will only be more and more and more pain and problems. Every time I see hope, something else awful would crush through.

I need to end it so I no longer suffer anymore. No more pain. No more black holes."

"I know," the time-travelling woman who was both a magic and fashion icon smiled at her. She still could not believe this woman was her, that they were the same person. *"It might seem impossible to have a future. I'm not going to lie to you. There is more pain that lies ahead, and more problems. We're a bisexual Chinese girl who has chronic mental illness and whose visa is constantly about to expire, in a foreign country where we got bullied growing up, but we grew up here for so long that we feel like our home country would not welcome us anymore. We are kind of right, even—some people weren't so welcoming. We are in between. We are the anomaly. Nothing will come easy, not for us."*

"Why, then?" She didn't realise tears starting to stream down her face. She snarled at the woman.

She was trying to convince her to live on while promising that this pain would never go away? Unbelievable. "Why should I carry on when I know it's just Hell on the other side? Why should I keep fighting a war I know I'm doomed to lose?"

"Well." Her future self let out a sad smile and said, *"That you have to find out for yourself. Who knows which version of the timeline your future self will step into?"*

"That could be nothing," she said. "My future could be the one where there is nothing."

"No, definitely not nothing," The woman shook her head and said, *"Because I am still here, which means you didn't go through with killing yourself. Regardless of which timeline you end up on, it wouldn't be the one where there is nothing. If that's the case, then none of the other uses would exist. You will live."*

"I will live," she repeated robotically. She put the container of pills down on the counter. "That one about being possessed by a supernatural entity and consulting ghosts for a living sounds interesting. Will I end up there?"

The woman rolled her eyes as if she could not believe what

she had just done. *"Seriously? That version of us is seriously messed up. I mean, she kind of needs more therapy than you do now."*

"You are not a particularly appealing version of where I want to end up in the future, either," she deadpanned. The light of the washroom felt warm, almost like a small sun was just born in this place that almost became her tomb.

"Ha!" The woman laughed loudly before bringing her into a huge bear hug. *"Then don't choose to become me, or any of those versions I mentioned earlier. They are all just possible timelines in the future for you. Death is boring, we all know where that road will lead. The future is chaotic and unpredictable. You'll never know unless you try."*

Judge of the Underworld Household

Bao Si Ran's dreams lead her into the underworld household.

The underground household she goes to is not Hell, nor is it the Greek Underworld ruled by Hades. It is called 阴朝地府 (Yin Chao Di Fu) in Chinese, which relatively translates to the Dynasty of Yin and the Underworld Court.

Depending on whether the person accumulated good or bad karma in life, one can either be sent immediately to their next life filled with joy, be promoted into a minor deity in the area, be a guardian ancestor for their family so people can build temples for them, or be given time to serve in the Underworld Household as punishment. But no one is trapped here forever, the King and Judge of the Underworld Household, 阎罗王 (The Yan Luo King), is always fair and impartial.

He cannot be bribed nor be coerced. He is the most just deity in the Chinese pantheon because while most other Heaven Officials are bureaucrats who are up their divine asses, Yan Wang never forgets about his duty.

Yan Wang told Si Ran once, "苍天无情—the Heaven has no

emotions. Those gods sit on their pedestals and receive sacrifices from the people on Earth. They only take and take; they don't know how it feels to have something taken from them. If one has no emotions, one cannot feel the pain and suffering of the victims. How can they deliver fair judgment without being burdened with feelings?"

Si Ran, who was taken from her country as a child and had practically no recollection of the mythology from her country, stood there and cried. She had just fallen asleep, and she thought she was in Hell.

There are people like Si Ran in the world, whose eyes could see into the world of the dead. In the daytime, it meant she could see ghosts. 阴阳眼, the eyes of Yin Yang, which meant she could see into worlds not of the living.

At night, however, it meant Si Ran's dreams could bring her to the Household of the Dead. There she met Yan Wang, the Judge of the Underground Household, her ancestor.

The first time she ever found herself walking into the Underground Household, she was only seven. It was a pretty place at first sight. Si Ran was delighted by All the poppy flowers with their lush redness at first. She thought it was just a dream, so her childish interest drove her to run into the poppy-coated shores and pick the flower. Very soon, she was holding a whole bouquet of poppies in her hands. Some of them fell and hit the Yellow Streams, and the broken pedals were washed away into the unending flows.

"Hey, child. Those aren't things you can just pick up!"

Si Ran turned her head when a harsh voice sounded behind her. At the sight of the creature that was yelling at her, Si Ran let out a cry and shook in horror. It had an ox's head and a human's body and was holding a trident pointed at Si Ran.

His tone was also quite rude, which made Si Ran burst out crying.

"Hey, hey. Child, don't cry." Ox Head said, panicked, as if Si Ran's response was not what he was anticipating.

"You scared the child," another creature said, her voice much calmer. If the Ox Head's voice was the harsh wind that blows through the poppy flower shores, hers was the gentle tug of the Yellow Streams. "Dead spirits of children are automatically sent to the Reincarnation Cycle. What are you doing here, little girl?"

Si Ran stopped crying, for she thought she had found an ally. But when her tears cleared from her eyes so she saw the true face of the gentle voice, she was scared back into her howling tears. The voice belonged to a creature with a horse head and a human body.

"Oh, great job, Horse Head." Ox's Head mocked his partner. "Because you're doing a much better job than me."

"Shut up." Horse Head sounded annoyed. "This child is alive. So she must be one of the Yan King's descendants. They sometimes wander into the Underworld mistakenly. Let's take her to him."

So they took Si Ran to the Yan King, kicking and screaming. "You're a fierce girl," the Ox Head complained. "How the hell did you not inherit the King's calm nature?"

Si Ran only kicked him in his Ox eyes in response.

She didn't remember much about that first trip to her ancestor's household. The only thing she remembered was the building's green roofs and red walls. It resided in the middle of the Yellow Streams which slowly grew into a lake. The interior design was simple and not lavish at all, despite the creatures claiming it was their king's residence.

In the middle of the room was a man in his late sixties. He had a dark complexion and very stern-looking eyes. Si Ran stopped crying upon seeing him because those eyes bore into her like two searing hot flames despite being as dark as the abyss. There was a moon symbol carved into the forehead of the old man.

"Sir, we found one of your descendants wandering around the Ming territories," Ox Head said. "It would be much appreciated if you tell them to … maybe not do that. It's annoying to care for humans who are alive; we already have a handful with the dead. If this carries on, we might demand a raise in salary."

"Ox Head," Horse Head muttered to him loudly enough for Si Ran to hear. "We don't get paid. Now stop disrespecting the Yan King."

"Sure, then we demand more breaks." Ox Head said.

"OX HEAD."

"I will take that into account," the man, Yan King, opened his mouth. His voice, surprisingly, was very ordinary. Despite the stern tone, it was a voice Si Ran could hear from anyone. "Go have your break. Leave us alone."

"Yes, sir," Ox Head and Horse Head said as they evaporated into smoke.

Si Ran let out a little yelp.

Yan King stood and walked closer. Si Ran scrambled backward instinctually. Seeing that, the Yan King stopped approaching Si Ran, instead moving backward to keep a safe distance between them.

"Sorry for the circumstances of our first meeting," the Yan King said. He sounded much more gentle and soft than when he was talking to the animal-headed creatures. "What is your name?"

"Si … Si Ran," the girl stuttered.

"Okay, Bao Si Ran," the Yan King said. "It is very nice meeting you."

"How do you know my family name?" Si Ran shivered. This couldn't be good.

"Because your father is the son of my son's son, give or take a few dozen generations," Yan Wang replied. "Only humans with my last name and blood can enter the Underworld in their dreams. "

"You ... are you the Devil?" Si Ran asked hesitantly. She was thinking of the Hell she learned of growing up.

"I don't know what that is, child," Yan Wang said patiently. A patient smile filled with wrinkles appeared on his face. "Judging by your tone, it seems to be something bad. If you are talking about Yao Guai, no, I am not a Yao Guai. Yao Guai are the spirits of animals or inanimate objects when they obtain a human level of consciousness. Even Yao Guais can be kind and good. It all depends on the route they choose. We can only judge people only by their conduct."

Si Ran, as a seven-year-old, didn't catch any of that. The only thing she remembered was that she was mesmerised by the matter-of-fact tone of the Yan King. He wasn't condescending in the way adults usually talked to her. As a child, that was all it needed for Si Ran to trust him.

"Okay," Si Ran said. "You seem nice."

"Thanks," Yan Wang said, "because you're going to see more of me in the future."

Sure enough, Si Ran did see more of Yan Wang. Sometimes she'd walk directly into one of Yan Wang's court sessions where he judged dead souls, where Si Ran would scream Yan Wang's name and run up to hug him while Ox Head scrambled after her to keep her out of the courtroom. Much to the dead soul's confusion, no less.

Sometimes she'd catch Yan Wang in some of his free time, which wasn't much considering how many people died all the time. During these precious times, Yan Wang would carry Si Ran up and let her ride on his back. She'd tug at Yan Wang's beard or the bead of his judge's hat and giggle. Yan Wang never stopped her. He would obey any of Si Ran's increasingly absurd demands, all to make the little girl smile.

The souls in Yan Wang's court were always shivering and afraid. Si Ran didn't understand how so. Yan Wang was such a pushover in her eyes, like the grandpa across the ocean that she had never met. Yan Wang would sometimes even allow her to sit next to her on his judge's seat as he delivered the verdict, as long as Si Ran promised to not stir and disrupt the court session.

"You can do whatever you want, Si Ran," he said. "My home is yours. But remember, a court session is something sacred and firm. Under no circumstances can you disrupt the procedure of the judgment. Because it could be a game to you, but to the soul, it is their entire life and afterlife at stake. I cannot make a mistake."

Si Ran nodded. As she grew up, she developed a reverence for the court and the justice system. She would sometimes demand her parents take her to court just to watch sentences being carried out, much to her parents' confusion. They didn't get why a little girl would be interested in sitting in a quiet and serious environment such as a courtroom for hours or even days on end, all while being as still as a rock.

However, once Si Ran became a bit older, she started to realise the sentences carried out in the courts of day time were very different from the ones in her ancestor's Underground Court.

One time when she was thirteen, she demanded Yan Wang take her to see where the punishment of the sentencing was carried out. Yan Wang appeared hesitant at first, but he could never deny any of Si Ran's requests, so he took her to some of the levels of the Underworld.

In one of these levels, souls were being boiled in hot oil. Si Ran gasped in horror as she heard the bubbling of skins bursting from the heat. The smell of roasted meat hung on her tongue but was accompanied by the howls of animals from human mouths. She couldn't help but bend down and vomit.

"Is this too much for a living child's eyes?" Yan Wang furrowed his brow. "Maybe we should go to the higher levels where the punishment is a bit kinder."

So he took Si Ran to the first level of the Underground Court, where people's tongues were being pulled as long as they could. The sound of sinews being stretched out like rubber bands with the veins popping out on the glowing red flesh made Sin Ran dizzy.

"How can you do this to people?" Si Ran asked as she could not believe what she was seeing. She was shaking like a leaf in the autumn wind. The grandpa that spoiled her rotten slowly morphed into a monster. "They are just people! My teacher said even the death penalty is wrong and immoral because we cannot be as bad as the people who do horrendous things. Let alone that - it's torture! No one deserves that."

Yan Wang looked at her carefully. There was a deep exhaustion in his eyes. "Child, you are just like the gods," Yan Wang said, his voice still kind but firm. "You know nothing of the suffering of the victims. The man you saw was roasted in hot oil. He lured and sold thousands of women fleeing from a country or poverty as sex slaves or wives to men who could pay the price. The person whose tongue was pulled out stole children from their parents and sold them to beggar organisations to garner sympathy from the pedestrians. He pulled out their tongues or crippled them. Do you know how many children disappear in the land of Hua Xia each year? Enough to fill the eighteen levels of the underground household. Compared to the millions of people they have hurt, only a few thousand are truly condemned to suffer in the Underground, most of them are let off free into the next life, though maybe as an insect or cattle due to bad karma."

"Maybe they do deserve it," Si Ran said. "But what if you are wrong? That's one of the reasons the death penalty is bad. It kills innocent people sometimes. And even if they are guilty, you who put them through that kind of torture, aren't you just as bad as them?"

Yan Wang shook his head. He looked older, as if the ages were catching up to him all of a sudden. "I am nothing but a judge, child." Yan Wang said, "If you think delivering punishment to people in equal measure to the pain they cause is wrong, then you must have your way. You grow up on a land not of your ancestors. You do not understand our philosophy or our law. 杀人偿命,天经地义. A life must be repaid by a life, such is the law of Heavens and Earth. Showing mercy to the perpetrator is the same as standing against the victims. You shouldn't come back until you learn the pain of the victims."

Si Ran was speechless. She was still stunned at the cruelty that her ancestor was capable of, let alone the fact that her dear grandpa was chasing her out of his territory. Yan Wang turned his back against her and waved his hand. Ox Head and Horse Head appeared to escort Si Ran out.

"You are such a stupid child!" Ox Head said as Si Ran walked numbly out, her eyes floating without focus. "How can you question the Yan King? You know how in five thousand years of Hua Xia history, he is the only one who gained the right to judge the souls entering into the Underground Household. Five thousand years, with Hua Xia's huge human population! You're just one girl. What makes you think you have the right?"

"Shush." Horse Head slapped Ox Head's head with the flat side of her axe. "Shut up. Can't you tell the little princess is already not in a good mood? It's between the girl and the Judge. Don't meddle in the boss' business."

Before she stepped through the portal and woke up, Si Ran turned her head up for a little bit and looked into Horse Head's eyes for the first time. "Thank you," she muttered quietly.

"No problem, little lady." Horse Head said kindly. "You make the Judge happy. In his long existence as the Yan King, you are the only descendant who stuck around enough to form a relationship with him. Judging dead souls is a tough job. You have to consider every single person's miserable life as your own to understand what they deserve. It is a tiring and thankless job, and one must be done well and not allow mistakes because a mistake destroys a life. Sometimes I think people living the world above forget that no matter how they paint him as a legend, Bao Zheng was just a human who was once alive."

"Bao Zheng?"

"That's the Yan King's name," Horse Head said. "Only humans can judge humans. Lady Si Ran. The Yan Wang before the Judge was cruel and unfair, who crossed out the names of people who gave him sacrifices and built him temples. That was why when Bao Zheng died, he was given this job. Only he can be the true judge of the underworld household."

One year led to the next. For years, Si Ran lived on without ever dreaming again. Her dreams would always lead her back to the Yellow Streams filled with poppy flowers, and a kind grandpa who delivered verdicts to souls.

She learned in those years, after going to university and studying law herself. Human laws could never be fair. Sometimes they would let go of guilty people on the sway of human biases or condemn the innocents based on their prejudices. Some judges and juries would give leeway to men who raped women instead of protecting the women, all to protect the men's futures. Some courts would destroy the lives of people who had a different shade of skin despite them never being in the wrong.

She witnessed all of it and learned that the crimes that are most unforgivable are those that went unpunished, when the victims' cries for help went unheard or ignored.

She might never agree with the method of her ancestor and the punishment he delivered, but she learned what he meant by the pain and suffering of victims.

The night she held her graduation certificate, Si Ran dreamed again. She saw a door open in front of her that led to the courtyard filled with poppy flowers, with a house that had a red roof and green walls.

A pair of monsters with ox and horse heads bowed their heads to her.

"Princess of the Underworld," they said to her, "the judge has missed you very much."

SEMYAZA
FROM THE
GHOST OF
ASH MONROE

TING
FROM THE GHOST OF ASH MONROE

Meet Your Demons

I.

The night slowly spit out its deafening despair, like a poisonous cloud that slowly engulfed one's mind. The sweet whipping cream she put on the waffle this morning became a greasy mess that now only made her want to vomit. Fear showered her nerves with a burning sensation. The demons that couldn't catch up to her in daylight suddenly swelled up like a pustule that one cannot scratch. If she thought about it too hard, then it would pop and leave a vicious scar that was doomed to torment her throughout the night. There is this thing about going to sleep—it makes one feel powerless. One cannot do anything in sleep except dream, which is practically useless. For someone who already felt powerless to control her life, night and sleep are another level of terror that completely devours one's agency.

So instead of falling asleep, Ting turned on the lamp and picked up a book that was lying limply on the ground after she had kicked it off the bed. If her psyche and health didn't require her to go to sleep for about seven hours a day, then Ting would probably spend the hours of the night awake. This time was the only part of the day that completely belonged to herself, with no expectations or interference from the sister who cared for her more than life. She also wouldn't have to face the reality of her situation; no one was left awake to remind her what she had to do or ask her what led her to where she was. The silence was perhaps the most blissful thing that had ever happened to Ting.

After two and a half hours, the words in the book started to fuse like a million ants, and Ting's eyelids began to throb. The complicated, tangled phrases and sentence structure caused a fiery prickle that hampered Ting's enjoyment. Classics were never light readings, and Ting never necessarily liked them. The plot was one that high schoolers would have known from literature class, but back then Ting never bothered to look at the original text. Now, it drew her like a magnet for some odd reason. That prickling feeling grew bigger as she tried to force the next paragraph into the back of her mind. If she were a child, then Ting would have been screaming for help because a monster was possibly in the closet.

However, Ting was not a child anymore. The monster in the closet would not find her worthy enough to taunt. She decided that the prickly feeling must have been the side effect of not being able to get a good night's sleep for about three nights already. Maybe she really should have tried to close her eyes and chase away the demons, though the effort seemed pointless now.

Whenever she closed her eyes, the thoughts that were temporarily suppressed by the words in her book would come back like a colony of bees.

She went to the bathroom and washed her face with some hot water to soothe her nerves. Her sister said it might help her insomnia; however, Ting thought it was only the advice of a desperate woman who had run out of suggestions for her sister to try to survive. Unfortunately, Ting was also desperate enough to believe her.

The mirror above the sink reflected the face of a ghost. Her hair was oily like the juice squeezed out of hamburger meat, dandruff among its mix shining like stars in the black mop. The skin on her face had been scrubbed with her pointy nails until it peeled off and revealed the pink and scarlet flesh underneath.

People wrinkled their noses when they noticed Ting's nervous smile and those self-inflicted wounds, but they couldn't feel a twinge of the nausea that overwhelmed Ting. They didn't seem to notice the screams of pain Ting's heart let out at the pressure of their gaze. They didn't hear how Ting begged God to let her go back to her room where there was no one else.

"Man, how long ago did you last step out of the house?"

At first, Ting only stared at her reflection with exhausted blankness. The words of disgusted judgment were nothing new to Ting's mind. They were so common that she almost found comfort in them like a dusty teddy bear. Those internal insults were the only things she could trust of herself anymore.

She didn't realise that it belonged to a completely separate entity until the reflection in the mirror began to morph.

"Come on. Your mind is so vulnerable for something sinister to creep in that I almost feel sorry for doing this."

Ting's mouth—no—the mouth of the reflection in the mirror began to curl up into a smile that was so wide that its edge touched its ears. Ting couldn't have managed the strength to smile so brightly even if she tried her hardest.

The black hair on Ting's reflection stretched from her scalp and curled up into waves of honey blonde. The vines on her face burned in a fiery scarlet as if they would start bleeding. But they didn't. Instead, those vines assembled into a dragon-shaped scar that covered half of her face. One last change occurred as Ting's black pupil began to expand until her entire eyelid became the same colour.

The woman that replaced Ting's reflection smiled back with

her cracked lips. Her teeth shot out of her mouth like stalactites from a cave.

Ting blinked thrice at this new development. *Ah,* the first thought flooded into her mind, *I am officially hallucinating. Does that mean I can officially be institutionalised and not deal with living at home?*

The reflection's face dropped instantly. It was not Ting's fault, as she remained expressionless at this sudden jump scare. Maybe that was why the ghost in the mirror was so pissed, because Ting's reaction wasn't what she was expecting.

"Come on!" the reflection growled in an animalistic voice. "There's a demon in the mirror. Can you at least pretend to appreciate the performance?"

Ting stared at the self-proclaimed demon blankly. A woman's voice was not usually that low.

"Why are you only focusing on my voice?" the demon questioned. Were she not a demon, it would have sounded like panic. "No reaction to the eyes? The teeth? Not even the fact that *your reflection just turned into something else?*"

Ting realised the demon could read her mind. That somehow made her feel relieved; communication was much easier this way, since she could not hide anything.

I didn't think it was polite.

The reflection in the mirror clipped the bridge of her nose with two fingers and closed her eyes. "You gotta be fucking kidding me," she murmured to herself in an almost offended voice. "I possessed a moron."

Those words make Ting flinch.

"Seriously?" The demon blinked twice at the sight of Ting's sudden change of manner. "You are not afraid of demonic possession, but apparently you're hurt by some mean words."

Ting only stared at her some more, this time with more tension.

"Okay, okay." The demon's breath hitched after being scrutinised by Ting's stare for about ten seconds. "I apologise. I didn't mean what I just said. You are pretty tough actually. Usually at this stage humans would either faint or start cursing in the Almighty's name. They'd actually be, *you know*, scared."

The demon looked at Ting again with an accusatory expression as if it was Ting's fault for not jumping out of the window. Ting couldn't help but crack up at this sight, which only seemed to infuriate the demon even more.

"Why are you laughing?" The demon's face darkened as she looked at Ting. "Is this funny to you?"

Yes, a bit, Ting found herself thinking.

"Please stop before I snap your neck in half."

Now she's embarrassed.

The demon was infuriated by those words. Her fangs grew longer as a result. "Oh for fuck's sake—I thought you were offended by humiliation. You humans are real hypocrites, you know?"

Ting's laughter came to a halt. The words drilled into her head by the demon started to sink in. It connected with those thoughts that came to her before in bed. They mixed into a bitter flavour in her mouth. She shut up, her expression becoming blank in a split second.

Ting could think of nothing else.

"You're feeling like you want to jump out of the window. Finally. Should have done that minutes ago." The demon's voice was cheerful and filled with honey as light and sweet as her hair.

I'm sorry.

"Wait, is that why you want to jump out the window?"

Erh, yeah? Ting changed her footing, wishing she didn't said anything more that might make the demon feel terrible.

"You completely missed the point." The demon rolled her eyes, finally giving up on informing Ting of her abnormal reaction to a demon., "Let's cut to the chase. You may not have noticed, but I am residing in your shadow. I have followed you a long time, so you have to know that trying to get rid of me is impossible—"

Poor demon, Ting thought. *I stayed in my house all the time. It's bliss for me, but it must be boring as hell for her.*

The demon twitched upon hearing Ting's inner voice. She wanted to have another outburst, but her better judgment told her it wouldn't get her anywhere with this human. "Boring is the wrong adjective." the demon said dryly. "Can we please focus?"

Yeah, sorry.

"I want to make a deal with you. A contract, if you prefer."

Ting was dumbfounded by those words. The demon's black eyes and deadly fangs finally caught up with her. Of course, why would a demon appear in her mirror? Did it want her soul? Maybe God had already realised what she planned to do, so He was dooming her to hell before she took action. Or maybe she was just unlucky. Wasn't that the most fitting summary for her entire resume? Something to trade for her soul. Maybe it was the best thing that could happen to her after all these years of solitude.

The demon had seen through her simple mind. She shook her head with the intensity of a rattle drum. "No, honestly, why do you humans always assume we will have any use for your souls?"

Erh, maybe decoration?

"No, girl." The demon planted her face in her palm. "More souls means more workload. I don't think *down there* needs any more contribution. Humans have already doomed themselves."

Ting's eyes sparked with a dark sense of curiosity. The demon quickly pulled the topic back to the details of this contract.

"I will fulfil three wishes if you offer yourself up as my vessel."

That doesn't sound so bad for a deal with a demon. There might be a trick, a disproportionate punishment after her three wishes. Or perhaps her wishes would be twisted according to the demon's interpretation and cause more harm than good for Ting. Those were the most common loopholes in stories touching on the topic of deals with an evil entity. However, something else bugged Ting more than those possibilities.

Ting spoke to the demon for the first time, "You are asking my consent for possession. A minute ago you were saying that trying to get rid of you would be impossible. Were you lying? Also … wait. Come to think of it, you said you are already possessing me. Does that mean I can repel you out of my body if I want?"

Through the bond, Ting could begin to understand the demon's thoughts, like a glimmer of sunlight on a lake.

Ting's voice was the sound of bells ringing on a Christmas night, or maybe a song from the Children's Choir. It reminded the demon of the waterfalls in Kaieteur, strings of silver hitting the rocks with a deafening intensity. The demon's head—if she had a physical head, that is - was overrun by an ache that was very similar to being burnt by hellfire. The urge to screech escaped the demon's throat like a sharpened knife. She was not expecting this sullen human who looked like she was approaching her death to have such a pure voice.

She hadn't spoken before, so the demon assumed that Ting's voice matched her life—a girl who confined herself in her narrow room whose heartbeat would rise at the very sound of boots outside her front door. A human who is mentally weak but had the wish to sin. It was the perfect combination to allow a demon's predatory form inside.

This first impression required reevaluation. This was the price to pay for underestimating others. She was now trapped in the body of someone who had the willpower and at least some intentions that fit the Father's taste to exorcise or confine the demon, not that the girl seemed to realise this yet. Ting's words were alarming enough for the demon to not lie again.

"Yes, you can," the demon said. She tried to dampen the sudden surge of regret, for she had realised Ting was sharp enough to recognize her lies. "But if it's any consolation, I will give you the advantage of proposing the details of the contract. My end of the deal is the same. As long as you agree to be my vessel, I can give you anything that you want."

"Are you desperate?"

"What?" The demon froze.

"No offence." The human finally looked into her eyes with a touch of light and concern, as if before she had merely been staring at her without seeing the demon's true form. "But you changed 'three wishes' to 'anything you want' pretty quickly. Are all demons this generous?"

The demon wanted to snarl at the human. Ting was getting on her nerves. The girl might have been smarter and more resilient than the demon originally thought, but if she wanted, she could still kill the girl in seconds.

Ting must have seen the murderous intent in the demon's pitch-black eyes. She didn't ask any further questions to provoke the demon's patience.

"Fine," Ting said simply, "I will agree to this if you will only take my body for eight hours a day. Those eight hours must be consistent. You will not harm any human during the possession either physically or mentally. Also, I will not be conscious for those eight hours of possession, and there better not be any consequences I have to bear in one way or another. Those are my three wishes."

"That's…" The demon lost any words she might have had before, "four wishes."

Oh, sorry. Ting thought.

Still, the camouflage of timidity did not fool the demon this time. What surprised her was that these four 'wishes' were more like rules rather than real wishes. They only limited the demon's potential instead of enhancing the human's reward. *What the hell?* In her long existence, the demon was rarely this confused.

"You sure that's all?"

Yeah, I guess?

"What about harming animals?"

I forgot about that. Please don't harm animals.

"What if I break the deal? Aren't you afraid that there will be repercussions?"

Unbelievably, the human started to *smile* again.

I don't think you're going to break the deal if I ask so many questions about the potential risks. I trust you won't take advantage of me.

The demon's head ached differently now.

"Let's just get it over with," the demon sighed before extending her left hand from the other side of the mirror. She looked tired for the first time tonight.

On the other side of the mirror, the demon's hand looked ordinary—pale but fair skin with fingers that were both thin and long.

Ting thought if the demon was human and had a physical body, then she would be fit to be a piano player. However, the minute the demon's hand touched the surface of the mirror and started to appear on Ting's side of reality, its shape changed.

Claws peeled out from the tip of the physical hand, claws that looked like the beak of a woodpecker. Dark, seaweed-coloured fur covered every inch of the enormous paw. In the physical world, the demon's form seemed much more monstrous.

"Afraid now?" the voice of the demon pierced through Ting's reverie.

She looked up to see the demon raising an eyebrow, the look on the demon's face almost challenging.

"No," Ting said in a normal tone, "just different."

The demon's black eyes expanded into two saucers, but she didn't say anything in return. Ting did not see the reason to further this conversation, so she held the demon's paw with a determined shake.

Nothing happened. No sudden marks burned into the body or violent screams. The only indication of the demon's control was the reflection in the mirror. It dissolved of all its particularity, returning to the gaunt Asian girl whose eyes flashed black for a split second.

2.

Semyaza wasted her first night in the human's body by walking out of the girl's house and getting stopped by her worried sister. For about eight hours, she repeated the same answers to the older woman. No, she wasn't trying to sneak out of the house to do something dangerous to herself.

"Please don't hate me." The older woman's eyes filled with tears while Semyaza grimaced at her. "I just want you to get better. If you go back to bed and close your eyes, then you must be able to fall asleep. You just need to try harder."

The demon would have strangled the woman if not harming humans were not part of her deal with her host.

Among the boogers and bubbling words Ting's sister spilled out, Samyaza tried to mimic the poker face the host seemed to have perfected. It only made her facial muscles hurt. Her attempt must only made Semyaza's contained impatience more obvious.

At the end of the endeavor, the woman was still crying as the first ray of sunlight wriggled its way into the room. It was then that Semyaza gladly relinquished control of the body, leaving her host to deal with the disastrous aftermath.

Ting's sister finally let Ting go without suspecting she was going to end herself. The first thing the human did was race into the bathroom and confront Samyaza in the mirror. The demon was picking at her nails, ignorant or perhaps simply indifferent to the situation.

"What did I say about *consequences*?" Ting hissed into the mirror with a drive that Semyaza wouldn't believe she had last night.

Samyaza shrugged her shoulders, unfazed. She could not let

the girl see that she was suppressing another headache augering into her skull. A shiver of pain coursed down her spine.

"You can't expect me to avoid all consequences. That is impossible if I am walking around in your skin."

"I don't care." Ting leaned into the mirror, every line of her face laid bare in front of Semyaza's view. "If you do anything that has any sort of consequences ever again, I am going to chase you out of my body."

Semyaza maintained her composure even under Ting's dire threat. "You can't," she said cooly, as if lying was something she is used to, "as long as you already agreed to let me in, then there is nothing you can do now."

"Then why did you not just torture me into letting you in?" Ting pointed out the flaw in the demon's logic as quickly as Semyaza came up with the lie, "It is not too hard, you know. I am quite mentally fucked up already. It wouldn't be that hard, right?"

It would be, Semyaza wants to say. *How come you do not realise that having the strength to resist demon possession requires a well of mental strength?* But she doesn't say it out loud, because the human was quite close to the edge of expelling already.

"Fine," Semyaza finally agreed. "It is your body, you can do whatever you want with it. But can I ask you one question? Why are you listening to what your sister wants? You're quite young for a human, but still, you're a perfectly legal adult in your terms. You're clearly more aware of your own situation than your sister. Why let her run her mouth?"

Ting paled before storming out of the washroom. Semyaza considered that as a meagre victory over her human host. It gave her a sense of contentment at the time, like a dose of human alcohol. What she didn't expect was that it came as fast as it went. The hangover that ensues is rarely worth it.

For the next few days, the demon kept to the contract by sneaking out from the window and the balcony, despite her urge to break a bone or so in Ting's sister's body. At least then she would not be able to stop Semyaza's intent of getting out of the house.

Since the girl's room was on the second floor, Semyaza always fell on her stomach. The demon's impervious nature made sure Ting's body was not harmed. However, climbing back through the window was truly a pain in the ass with a human body. Semyaza's instincts told her this was inefficient. She didn't have that much time to obey the host's wishes. After all, she needed to hunt down her brother before his next kill.

Semyaza tried to persuade her host into giving her more leeway with the rules, but the stubborn creature just wouldn't budge.

After two weeks, Ting finally had enough and stopped looking into any mirrors altogether. This resulted in her sister's hysterical claim that Ting must be seeing things in the mirror.

Ting's sister wasn't technically wrong. She just didn't know what she was talking about. The human was unconscious during possession, but Semyaza was not when Ting was walking around. The more Semyaza stayed in the back of the human's head and observed her life, the more she did not understand how the human could be in her present state—trapped in a house with a crazy woman who thought Ting was crazy. The girl was smart. Just take a look at the books she read: *Frankenstein* and *Paradise Lost,* classics that Ting claimed were not her taste. Well, she clearly seemed like someone who liked to torture herself with a lot of things she claimed she doesn't like.For example this house, her sister, the classics, and Semyaza herself.

Another night approached the quiet suburban neighborhood. As Ting's consciousness slowly faded into sleep, Semyaza took the shift with a distinct feeling in her — well, *Ting's* — chest. The familiar touch of another supernatural being shone with a hellish amber that almost scorched Semyaza's senses.

A few hours ago, she threatened the human with death to let her take control, but Ting didn't waver at all. Besides, Semyaza was too distracted by her own thoughts to keep up the act of a terrifying demon.

A few months ago, Semyaza started hearing her brother's calling, she expected some heavenly host obeying the Father's command would come down and solve the problem. The voice in her head was practically sweating bloodthirst for human lives like a squeezed sponge of water. She couldn't believe that the Father who cast them out of Heaven in favour of the humans would practically turn a blind eye to this kind of outrageous behaviour. She thought if she stayed out of this, she wouldn't feel the possible responsibility of responding to the calling of her favourite sibling.

Contrary to her wish, the voice only grew louder and louder. It slowly became more and more impatient. It screamed at Samyaza with a voice that made her eyes bleed saying that he would prove to her that he was not some trap set by Father, but instead a friendly hand who wanted to repair their kinship after millennia of separation.

Semyaza didn't answer the call, obviously, just like any human who would avoid awkward family gatherings where one must meet cousins who became drug dealers somewhere down the line. What she didn't—or rather didn't *want* to—take into account was the possibility of Azazel having a temper tantrum. They really had similar tempers.

Then bodies started to turn up all along the places where Semyaza's vessels lived. He chased, so Semyaza ran, jumping from place to place. Finding a new vessel requires time and persuasion. Also, if one considered the host's mental health, then it was even harder to keep up with the clock.

Azazel clearly didn't have any concern with the way he left behind a trail of bodies that both filled up the local mortuary and mental asylums. Semyaza couldn't risk it, not with Azazel on her heels. At least, that was what she told herself.

Ting was a gamble. She was the most vulnerable individual in the area for Semyaza to get into, but the girl could somehow still retain her agency. No matter how much Ting wasted her potential, Semyaza's foolhardiness was rewarded by a host who wouldn't go crazy upon her departure. This was someone she could use to face Azazel ... without feeling sorry.

Again, that was what she told herself.

Samyaza had to get to Azazel before another human turned up dead.

She followed the scent of sulphur along the winding road. Some houses along the pitch-black street overflowed with loud metal music, laughter, and disco lights. The volume turned the demon away, as it is impossible even for Azazel to hurt anyone in such a large crowd while possessing a single human.

"Aw, that is such an underestimation of my ability. You should be ashamed of yourself, sister."

Her head exploded. Literally. Semyaza could not fathom as her - *Ting's* - brain burst like a smashed watermelon before she even turned around. The pure shock resulted in a screech that pierced Heaven before Semyaza even realised that she must still have vocal cords to shout.

Illusions, those were always Azazel's favourite. He liked to use it to torment his victims in Hell, but it worked on Semyaza, too.

"If you're wondering why I can catch you off guard, Ouza, it's because you're becoming too human"

Semyaza swept through the street with blurry vision. In the darkness, a fluffy amber cloud doused in light pounced into the street.. It was an elegant tabby cat, a harmless, cuddly toy. To Semyaza's tear-obscured eyes, however, it resembled a blossom of hellish flame..

"You're somehow so much better, Azazel. They say we turn into what we are. And you're nothing more than an animal right now." The demon bared her teeth before she realised Ting's teeth were not at all threatening.

The cat smirked impossibly. Semyaza stood her ground with caution before she felt something viscous dripping from her body.

She saw the world slowly dropping in height and found her lower limbs slowly detaching themselves, dissolving into a puddle.

"Is this all you can do, brother? I know it's not real. You can't hurt me."

"Can I not?"

Ting began to scream. Semyaza never heard such an inhuman sound in her long life. The bells on Christmas night broke into sirens from an air raid that bombarded an entire city. The children's choir turned into babies screaming for their mothers as they were slaughtered. The splashing water of Kaieteur Falls boiled when those bubbles of heat engulfed her trachea. Ting screamed and screamed, while Semyaza could do nothing but be confined to the side.

"Stop, please, Azzy. Please *stop*."

She begged without dignity. Semyaza could not face what was happening t. She begged her brother to stop as Ting's life drained from her body.

The girl might have wasted her potential, but Semyaza liked her. She was intelligent, stubborn, and self-destructive. She reminded Samyaza so much of herself. However, the human had something she did not—Ting was brave enough to face and love her sibling when Semyaza could only run.

"Azzy, I'm sorry," she murmured despite the pain. The realisation hit her like a divine punishment. "I am sorry that I left you in Hell all those years ago. I wish we could start again, together."

The hallucination dimmed for a moment as if stage lights had been cut. Semyaza's breath hitched at the sudden relief. The form Azazel possessed became clear for the first time. It was a rather chubby tabby cat, came a hazy, untimely thought into Samyaza's mind.

"You're not lying." It was a statement rather than a question, Azazel's voice filled with childish joy as he scrubbed his furry neck on Semyaza's legs. "Glad to have you back, dear sister."

3.

The demon looked like a six-year-old who had been caught stealing cookies from the jar. Although Ting realized the monster had only been a facade, she remained nervous. Semyaza buzzed through the explanation.

"Sorry, can you repeat everything you just said from the beginning?" Ting asked.

"Look ... I know you won't agree. After all, it's not part of the contract, but please think of the human lives at stake here, they're your kind—"

"No, I just didn't hear what you just said."

"Oh."

This time she managed a stronger voice. Ting nodded as the demon explained everything from beginning to end, including her request for Ting. Ting developed a newfound understanding of the demon's desperation when they had first met.

"Okay."

The demon stared at Ting, dumbfounded at her simple, crisp answer. Ting had become the supernatural creature, the oddity.

"Just like that?" the demon's black eyes narrowed into two ink lines, "No refusal? No bargains? Hell, no *questions*?"

"Could it hurt my sister?"

"No, not really." The demon shook her head blindly, still looking like she was walking in a dreamland. "You might die, though. Azazel will take complete control over your body. But I will make sure your sister is safe."

"Then ... okay." Ting shrugged.

"Seriously?" The demon's face dropped, but Ting the relieved smile she was suppressing underneath. "Do you never look out for yourself, Ting? No wishes you just want to fulfil purely for your own sake?"

That was the first time the demon had used her name. Ting smiled back.

"I *do* look out for myself," she answered truthfully. "This whole demon possession thing takes my mind off my problems. How much I owed my sister, for example. You helped with my insomnia, too. Almost forgot about how good it feels like to sleep for a whole eight hours before we made our deal. Believe it or not, dealing with people is somehow ten times scarier for me than dealing with you."

The demon was stunned. She opened her mouth to say something but closed it immediately afterwards. Her fanged mouth twisted as if trying to stifle a wail.

If this much is enough to shut her up, Ting thought, *then what I am about to do next will probably make her blush.*

"What do you - " The demon furrowed her brows in alarm. She never finished her sentence.

Ting's face leaned into the mirror. This time, she didn't hold back. The mirror's transparent surface clouded from the warmth of a human's breath. Once lifeless as a crypt, now it became light as a feather. In no way could it be considered a kiss. The demon's black eyes enlarged. She attempted to pull away due to shock. Given her two-dimensional state of being, that was proven impossible.

The human's lips connected with the reflection of her demon's. For a split second, the two beings collided. Fused into one.

They were each other's mirror.

"Thanks for showing me I am worth something," Ting said, letting the demon go for the last time.

4.

The ground beneath her feet was slowly disintegrating into silver-lined clouds. The cold breeze carried her honey hair up in a gentle swift of hands. Semyaza closed her eyes to the familiar yet cruel image that was unfolding in front of her.

Light started to fill in every corner of her being. It was not the illumination cast on stone walls by the lake of fire. There, brightness was always followed by endless shadow. Now, pure white light shone—the kind of light only mortals who have been true and just in life would see after Death decides to have their way.

Out of curiosity, she attempted to move her limbs. Her arms spread out. Human hands with pale, healthy skin had replaced her monstrous claws. The clouds tickled her bare, human feet.

Those were miraculous sights, but what truly made her heart flip was the swirling movement her body made as she hung in thin air. Her wings had returned, perfect as if they had never been ripped from her. They would carry Semyaza wherever she wanted to go.

"You remember when Father poured blue paint into the sky? Everyone protested, This is not fair! Now we're never going to find Ouza when we're playing hide and seek.' " His voice grew sorrowful, "They say the blue jays were modelled after you."

The voice of the creator—no, not the Creator—but the one who made this view possible appeared. Semyaza observed her surroundings with an ache that had been long forgotten. Azazel descended from the pearly gates, his illusion while looking adoringly at his sister.

"Very nice for you to say." Semyaza searched her brother's eyes for a flicker of something else. "Odd, too. Aren't you going to give yourself your wings back in this little make-believe world you created?"

"It won't be important," Azazel said with a wave of his hands, his smile growing wider. "I do not need something that was given and taken away at someone else's will."

"Yet somehow you think I would want these fuckers for the same reason. You've always been such a hypocrite, brother."

Semyaza smirked viciously at Azazel, again bearing her flat teeth.

The other demon's brows furrowed. "What are you indicating, Ouza?" His words were calm, but the danger laced underneath was undeniable. "I thought you wanted to get along."

The sudden shift in gravity pulling her down was expected, but instinctively Semyaza still struggled for a few moments for a handhold.

She screamed when the Fall began. Fire licked at her wings. It left them looking far too similar to human food, to greasy wings dripping with fat, piled high for gluttons.

"I know this is not real, Azazel!" her voice cracked despite Semyaza's best effort to stay calm. Everything was under control. She just needed to wait. "This can't get you what you wanted!"

"What do you mean by that?" Azazel's voice came from all directions. It would be amusing to see how much her brother had developed a God complex if Semyaza were not currently living her worst nightmare. "It was you who suggested we inhabit this human's body together and create any world we desire. We may not be able to control Heaven or Hell; Father and Lucifer have absolute power in both places. But here, *here* we can build our own kingdom, even if it's just a facsimile. Don't you want to have a life with me?"

The emotions of that last sentence dripped with sadness. Semyaza gulped. Her heart burned with both the desire for this falling simulation to stop and the lingering question she held about this plan.

"I do, Azzy," Semyaza said, tears burning when they left her eyes, "but I do not want a world where you are God. I will live on my own terms, not as the mere follower of you or Father or

Lucifer or anyone. I love you, but you can never sacrifice all of yourself in the name of love."

As those words ran from her mouth, it was almost like a new kind of light engulfed Semyaza's mind. It was not like Heaven's light or Hell's fire. It was anything but an imposter like Azazel. It was real. It was more of the ringing of bells on Christmas Eve, or Children's Choir singing on the shoulder of the Kaieteur mountains before jumping down. It belonged to the human who controlled her own body—where Azazel's illusions truly resided.

So, Semyaza trusted her human to give her strength. She flapped her wings furiously, creating a wind funnel to carry her up. Pure joy sang in her lungs just like it did before the fall. Back then, she was naive and good. Now, she is anything but.

"*How?*" Azazel's eyes filled with shadow. He could no longer maintain his desired form. "Someone is tampering with my illusions. That's not possible."

"It's not about reality," Semyaza said as her blue feathers blended into the sky beyond, "but in this body, everything is under the control of its owner alone. Here, brother, you are powerless."

"So what?" Azazel gleefully dissolved himself into a stream of smoke. "I just have to get out of this human's body to use my power."

"Afraid that's not possible, Azzy." Semyaza looked lazily at the swirling black smoke as it churned with anxiety. "Ting has the strongest mind of any human being I've possessed. Honestly, it gave me a headache, how she refuses to use it that often. She can repel or trap any supernatural being. So it's just you and me, brother dearest."

"What do you plan to do, Ouza?" Azazel laughed mockingly, "Kill me? You can't. I am your brother, after all."

"I know," Semyaza said, the smile disappearing from her face. "That is possibly the only reason I am doing this. My power will cancel out yours, Azazel. I love you, but I also love myself."

The black cloud exploded. The illusion of heaven disappeared as hellflame started to devour everything around them. Semyaza closed her eyes. Her wings turned to ash under the scorching heat. For a moment, the demon thought she saw the Creator wearing Ting's face. Smiling down after centuries of silence.

5.

"Where are you going?"

"Leaving."

"What? You can't just leave! You're going to be more anxious and you will come back-"

"I won't be back for a long time."

Her sister blocked the front door with her shaking frame. Ting extended her hand, she couldn't deny that her heart hurt when her sister flinched at her touch.

Ting pushed her sister aside. Her sister would never accept that she was only making Ting's mental state worse by imprisoning her in the house.

"I love you, sis." Ting smiled as her sister almost fainted at her rebellious gesture.

The sun shone on the suburban streets. Ting didn't know if the shadows would start to cloud her mind again tonight when the golden orb pulled away. She guessed the insomnia wouldn't go away overnight. It had become a habit, getting anxious whenever the sun went down, as if it were the end of all hope.

It's fine, though, Ting thought while she combed her black hair in the mirror. *Your demon is not that scary once you get to know them. Isn't that right?*

In the mirror, a figure with burn scars and blonde hair had her eyes closed. She had used up too much of her energy, so all Ting could do was hope the demon had a good night's sleep until she decided to wake up.

Acknowledgments

I have been writing the stories in this book throughout the last few years of my life. They range from my uni short stories assignment to my mid-breakdown coping mechanism writing. Horror to me is in a way comforting, as the acknowledgement of the society we live in is in a way mundane horror and to write through that lens from an Chinese queer diaspora perspective is what I realize underlines almost everything I wrote. Throughout this anthology, and my upcoming novel "From the Ghost of Ash Monroe".

The following people are the ones who I must thank for making this anthology a reality:

My editor and proofreader, Moth Hawke, who made my writing more coherent to the reader. Thank you so so much.

My amazing formatting artist, Lauren Cooper, you made this book's interior spooky and transformed what would otherwise just be a word doc into what this book is. Thank you for your patience and talent.

My friend Roshen, who is the amazing artist responsible for the character art of "Meet Your Demons", he truly brought Semyaza and Ting to life with his art in a way I didn't think was possible. I am infinitely grateful I manage to meet you through the book community on Instagram, being the cover designer and character artist of my upcoming novel "From the Ghost of Ash Monroe" where Ting and Semyaza are featured with larger roles, that book and this story's amazing character visuals will not exist without you. Also thank you for always believing in my writing, even when I do not believe in them myself.

The cover designer of this anthology, 麻辣月亮 (her lofter ID), who I probably need to send a Chinese translation of this acknowledgement to. Her cover truly brought the cozy horror vibe in my mind to become the clothes of my stories. The haunted house in the woods vibe on a sunny noon day is fantastic.

I also really want to thank Meg/Night for always being the best friend and reader one can hope for! Also a fellow BIPOC writer whose writing is absolutely beautiful. And Em, who was always there to read my stories.

On that list there are also all my arc readers: Sofia, Elysian, Manon, CeCe, Annie, Karnam, Ian Tan (陈颖), The Fall Reader, Aseel, Anne, Ket, Solace In Literature, Val, Theo, Brianna, Georgia, Sam, Azrah, Elena/ 迎芳 , Helena, Niki, Mella, Michelle, J C, Becca, Harvey, Carly, Gee, Lyn, Louis and Rian. Thank you for being interested in reading these pieces of stories that came from my disturbed mind.

My little sister, Charlotte, who probably is not the age to read something like this but if she manages to get access to this book, I just want to put her down here because I want to say sorry but also tell her I have been obsessed with horror from her age too. So don't fear, let it be a part of your imagination. But don't let Mom or Dad know. Okay?

Also here is to thank all of the readers of my Chinese stories, even though they might never read this anthology and probably never see this dedication. But without them and their support I would not have continued writing until now to make this book happen. They were what kept my creative flame alive and made me feel like my words meant something to someone. They made me from simply being someone who writes into a writer whose stories are perceived. So I will forever be grateful to their support, it feels unfair to leave them out of the first English book I ever put out.

Also By Dawn Chen:

From The Ghost Of Ash Monroe

The Witch Who Chases The Sun

Author Bio

Dawn Chen is a first-generation Chinese diaspora indie author who grew up in Beijing, China. When she was thirteen, she moved to Germany to live with her family. Since then, she has both lived in Canada and UK. She has a Bachelor's Degree in Law and Humanities (Qualifying Degree), but finds that writing fiction suits her better because she wants to escape reality.

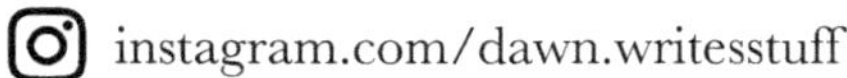 instagram.com/dawn.writesstuff

9 781738 491704